HarperCollins®, ♣®, and HarperFestival®
are trademarks of HarperCollins Publishers Inc.
The Tall Book of Nursery Tales
Illustrations copyright © 2006 by Aleksey & Olga Ivanov
All new material copyright © 2006 by HarperCollins Publishers Inc.
Manufactured in China. All rights reserved.
For information address HarperCollins Children's Books, a division of HarperCollins Publishers,
1350 Avenue of the Americas, New York, NY 10019
Library of Congress catalog card number: 2004107735
www.harperchildrens.com
Book design by Joe Merkel
1   2   3   4   5   6   7   8   9   10
❖
First HarperFestival edition, 2006

The Tall Book of Nursery Tales

ILLUSTRATED BY ALEKSEY & OLGA IVANOV

ADAPTED BY RAINA MOORE

HarperFestival®

A Division of HarperCollinsPublishers

Table of Contents

LITTLE RED RIDING HOOD

Once upon a time there was a little girl who lived in a cozy cottage near the edge of the woods with her mother. The girl liked to wear a red cloak with a hood. In fact, she wore it so much that soon she was known as Little Red Riding Hood.

One day her mother said, "Little Red, your grandmother is very sick. Bring her this basket of goodies but be very careful. Keep to the path and no matter what don't talk to strangers."

Little Red Riding Hood kissed her mother on the cheek. "Don't worry, Mama. I'll run all the way to Grandma's without stopping."

Little Red stayed on the path and spoke to no one . . . until she saw a bush full of raspberries. Raspberries were her grandma's favorite! She began picking berries, unaware that a wicked wolf was watching her from the woods.

"What a nice snack she will make," the wolf said under his breath. Just as he was about to pounce, the wolf heard the chopping sound of a woodsman working nearby. "Drat!" he muttered. He needed a plan.

"Where are you going, my pretty girl, all alone in the woods?" the wolf asked, with a toothy grin.

Little Red was so excited about the berries that she forgot her mother's warning. "To see my grandmother!"

"Have you far to go?" asked the wolf.

"Yes," said Little Red Riding Hood. "Her house is all the way on the other side of the woods."

"Well, then," the wolf said, with a little bow. "You had better be on your way."

Little Red Riding Hood skipped down the trail. But the sneaky wolf knew a shortcut. He dashed through the woods until he was at Grandma's door.

Knock! Knock!

"Who's there?" cried Grandma from her bed.

"It's me," said the wolf, trying to make his voice sound soft and sweet. "It's Little Red Riding Hood. I've brought you a basket of goodies."

"Come in," said Grandma.

The door opened, and a horrible shadow appeared on the wall. "Oh, my!" was all the poor old woman could say as the wolf leapt across the room and grabbed her. He tied her up with rope and put her in the closet.

The wicked wolf put on Grandma's nightclothes and climbed into her bed. Moments later, there was a knock on the door.

"Grandma," called Little Red Riding Hood, "may I come in?"

The wolf tried to imitate Grandma's quivering voice. "Come in!"

Little Red opened the door and set the basket down, and came closer. "Why, Grandma," she said, "what a deep voice you have."

"The better to greet you with," said the wolf.
"And what big eyes you have."
"The better to see you with."
"And what big teeth you have!"
"The better to *eat* you with!"

The wolf grabbed the girl and let out a sinister howl! His howl was so loud that it echoed through the woods. The woodsman, fearing the worst, grabbed his axe and ran toward the terrible noise. He burst through the door and found Little Red in the wolf's clutches. The woodsman swung his axe! The wolf jumped back, the blade just barely missing him, and let Little Red go.

"I'll get you next time," he said before running off into the woods.

Little Red Riding Hood ran to the closet and untied her grandma as the woodsman looked on.

Later, the three sat down to enjoy the goodies Little Red had brought . . . and she never, ever, *ever* spoke to a stranger again!

THE COUNTRY MOUSE AND THE CITY MOUSE

There was once a happy little mouse that lived in the country. In the summer, the country mouse scampered around the wheat field, eating grain whenever he felt like it. As the weather grew cold, the little mouse moved into the farmhouse. Inside he gathered nuts and barley that were dropped on the kitchen floor. When winter came, he had a good supply of food in three neat piles: one for nuts, one for barley, and one for crumbs.

One snowy winter day, there was a knock at the door. It was his cousin, all the way from the city! When the little city mouse sat down to dinner, he couldn't believe the country mouse had nothing to eat except barley, nuts, and crumbs.

The city mouse shook his head and said, "My poor country cousin. You do not live well at all. Why, you should see how I live! I have fine things to eat every day."

The country mouse immediately felt ashamed of his simple home.

The city mouse went on, "Tomorrow, we'll go to the city. I'll show you my home and you will see how much nicer it is where I live."

In the morning, they went to the city where the houses were big and there were people everywhere.

The very first place that the city mouse took his cousin was the kitchen cupboard. Inside there was a sack of brown sugar. They began to eat at once. The country mouse had never tasted anything so delicious in his life!

"Wow, cousin," the country mouse said. "You are so lucky!"

Just then, the door swung open with a bang. The city mouse ran for the hole in the corner of the cupboard but the country mouse froze with fear. A cook reached into the cupboard and to her surprise came nose to nose with the country mouse.

She let out a scream and dropped the flour on the floor.

"Don't just stand there, cousin!" shouted the city mouse. "Come on!"

The country mouse scurried through the little hole. When they were safe, the country mouse said, "Whew! That was close."

The city mouse dusted the flour off his whiskers. "Don't worry. She'll be gone soon and then we can go back."

After the cook had gone away, they crept back to the kitchen. This time, the city mouse had something new to share. They went through the hole in the cupboard, where a big jar of dried cherries was left open. These were even better than the brown sugar! Everything was wonderful until they heard *scratch, scratch, scratch* on the cupboard door.

"What is that?" asked the country mouse.

Suddenly there was a loud meow!

The city mouse ran as fast as he could to the hole, and this time the country mouse followed.

As soon as they were out of danger, the city mouse said with a glint in his eye, "That old cat will never catch me! Let's go down to the pantry. There is even more food down there!"

Down in the pantry, there were rounds of cheese, bunches of sausages, and barrels full of pickles. It smelled so good that the little country mouse went wild. He scurried around the room, nibbling a little cheese here and a bit of a pickle there, until he saw a morsel of cheese on a strange little stand in a corner. He was just about to take a big, healthy bite when the city mouse saw him.

"Stop!" cried the city mouse. "That's a trap!"

The little country mouse stopped in his tracks. "What's a trap?"

"That *thing*," said the little city mouse, "is a trap. The minute you touch the cheese, something comes down on your head hard, and—" The city mouse made a loud *clap* with his little hands.

The little country mouse looked at the trap. Then he looked at his cousin. "I think I will go home," he said. "I'd rather have barley and grain and eat it in peace, than have brown sugar and cheese and eat in fear."

The two mice shook hands. The country mouse happily went back to his home. And there he stayed for the rest of his life.

The Gingerbread Man

Once upon a time, there was a little old woman and a little old man, and they lived in a little old house. They didn't have any children of their own but wished for a son. So one day the woman decided to make a boy out of gingerbread! She took a bit of spicy dough, rolled it thin, and cut it into the shape of a boy. She gave him a chocolate jacket, two raisins for eyes, and a smile made of rose-colored sugar. With a little pat, she popped him into the hot oven. "Now I will have a boy of my own!" she said.

When it was time for the gingerbread boy to be done, she opened the oven door. Just as she was reaching in, the gingerbread boy sprang from the oven.

"Come back!" the old woman shouted.

The gingerbread boy just laughed and laughed. "Run, run as fast as you can. You can't catch me— I'm the gingerbread man!" And he was right; she could not catch him.

The gingerbread boy ran into the yard with the old woman close behind him. He ran past the old man chopping wood.

"Come back!" the old man shouted, but the gingerbread boy just laughed and laughed.

"Run, run as fast as you can! You can't catch me—I'm the gingerbread man! I've run away from the little old woman, and I can run away from *you*. I can, I can!" With the old man and the old woman not far behind him, the gingerbread boy dashed into the woods.

He ran on, until he came to a cow chewing grass. The cow eyed the gingerbread boy hungrily. "Come back!" the cow shouted, but the gingerbread boy just laughed and laughed.

"Run, run as fast as you can! You can't catch me— I'm the gingerbread man! I've run away from a little old woman and a little old man, and I can run away from *you*. I can, I can!"

The cow ran as fast as she could, but she couldn't catch him.

The little gingerbread boy ran on, until he came to a bear picking berries. The bear stopped eating and imagined what a nice snack the gingerbread boy would make.

"Come back!" the bear shouted, but the gingerbread boy just laughed and laughed.

"Run, run as fast as you can! You can't catch me—I'm the gingerbread man! I've run away from a little old woman, a little old man, a cow chewing grass, and I can run away from *you*. I can, I can!"

The bear ran as fast as he could, but he couldn't catch him.

By and by, the gingerbread boy came to a field full of farmers. When the farmers smelled the gingerbread boy, they tried to pick him up, but the gingerbread boy ran faster than ever!

"Run, run as fast as you can! You can't catch me—I'm the gingerbread man! I've run away from a little old woman, a little old man, a cow chewing grass, a bear picking berries, and I can run away from *all* of you. I can, I can!"

And the farmers couldn't catch him.

The gingerbread boy bounded through the woods, not realizing that a hungry fox was looking on.

"You should be more careful, little cookie," the fox said.

But the gingerbread boy was not afraid. "Run, run as fast as you can! You can't catch me—I'm the gingerbread man! I've run away from a little old woman, a little old man, a cow chewing grass, a bear picking berries, a field full of farmers, and I can run away from you. I can, I can!"

"I do not wish to catch you," the fox said with a grin. "On the contrary, I want to help you. You see, there is a river just ahead. I will give you a ride across on my tail so that the others cannot reach you."

The gingerbread boy heard the thumping of feet running to catch him. He looked at the river. Then he made his decision.

"Kind fox," he said, "since your tail is so far from your mouth, I accept the ride."

The gingerbread boy jumped on the fox's tail, and the fox started across the river. The fox swam for a while, then said, "Oh, my! The water has grown deeper. Hop on my back, gingerbread boy, or you will get wet."

So the gingerbread boy jumped from the fox's tail to his back.

A little farther out, the fox said, "Oh, dear! The water has grown even deeper. You will surely get wet if you stand there. Why don't you jump on my shoulder?"

So the gingerbread boy jumped from the fox's back to his shoulder.

In the middle of the stream, the fox said, "Oh, no! Now the water is *very* deep. Quick, jump on my head so that you don't get wet!"

So the gingerbread boy jumped from the fox's shoulder when, suddenly, the fox threw back his head, opened his mouth, and *snap*! The gingerbread boy was gone.

CINDERELLA

Once upon a time, there was a girl called Ella whose mother lay sick in bed.

"Dear child," Ella's mother said, "promise me you'll always be good and kind."

With her father beside her, Ella held her mother's hand. "I promise, Mama," the young girl said.

Just then, her mother drew her last breath. Ella felt her father's arm wrap around her shoulder, and together they cried.

A year passed, and Ella's father was ready to marry once again. He met a widowed lady who had two daughters, Lucretia and Gunilla. At first the lady was pleasant and made Ella's father very happy. But as soon as the wedding was over, the new wife began to show her true colors. She was haughty, spiteful, mean, and rude—and her daughters were exactly like her.

The stepmother gave Ella many chores to do.

"When you finish cleaning the fireplace" the wicked stepmother shouted, "you *must* feed the pigs and scrub the floor!"

"Yes, Stepmother," Ella replied, her face and hands smudged with gray from the ashes in the fireplace.

Lucretia pointed at Ella's face and laughed. "Look at how dirty she is from the cinder ashes!"

"Why, she's Cinderella," said Gunilla, giggling the whole time.

From then on, they always called her Cinderella. Cinderella's clothes were rags, while her stepsisters had fine dresses. Cinderella slept on a straw bed near the kitchen, but her sisters had big rooms and soft beds. But all that didn't matter. Even dressed in tattered clothes, Cinderella was kind and delicate, loyal and sincere. No matter how cruel her stepmother and sisters were, Cinderella remained good—just as she had promised her mother.

One morning, as Cinderella was scrubbing the floors, a messenger came to announce the prince's ball. Her stepsisters jumped up and down with joy, each thinking she had a chance to marry the prince. The ball was days away but they immediately started choosing gowns to wear.

"Cinderella," Lucretia said, with a haughty smile, "wouldn't you like to go to the ball?"

"Well, yes, I would."

"But what would you wear?" Gunilla asked. "A dress made of ashes and straw?"

At this the sisters twisted their faces into mocking smiles and began to laugh. Cinderella looked away in shame.

At last the happy day arrived. The stepsisters spent the entire day dressing in front of the mirror. But no amount of fabric could hide the ugliness deep in their hearts. Cinderella watched their carriage leave. As soon as it was out of sight, she fell to the floor and cried.

Just then, in a beam of splendid light, a kindly old woman appeared.

"Why are you crying, child?"

Cinderella was stunned. "Who are you?"

"I am your fairy godmother, here to grant you what you most desire. You would like to go to the ball, wouldn't you?"

"Yes," the girl replied. "More than anything!"

"You shall have your wish," said her godmother. "But I will need a few things. Let's see . . . a pumpkin, six mice, two lizards, and, hmm . . ." she thought for a moment, tapping her magic wand on her chin. "Oh, yes, a rat."

Cinderella ran around the garden collecting these things, but how on earth were they going to get her to the ball?

The fairy godmother waved her wand, and the pumpkin was instantly turned into a golden coach!

She whirled her wand above the mice, and they became six proud horses. With a flick of her wrist, the fairy godmother shot a magic beam of light at the rat, and he became a coachman to drive the carriage. She twirled her wand around the lizards, and suddenly there stood two footmen, whose job it was to help a lady step in and out of a carriage.

Cinderella was overwhelmed with joy. "But I have nothing to wear."

With a twinkle in her eye, her godmother ever so lightly touched the girl with her wand. In an instant, her clothes were turned from sooty rags to fine silk. Surely it was a dream! But no—this was real!

Cinderella looked down at her feet. "Glass slippers?" she asked.

"That's right. But come now. It is time for you to go. And remember, you must be home at midnight. If you stay one moment longer everything will return to what it was."

Cinderella promised to leave the ball before midnight. "Thank you!" she said, hugging her fairy godmother. With that, she boarded her coach and was off to the ball!

Cinderella arrived at the ball and followed the happy music up the grand staircase. But as soon as she entered the room, there was a strange silence. People stopped dancing and the violins ceased to play, for everyone in the room was mesmerized by her beauty.

The prince approached Cinderella and offered his hand. The music started and together they danced . . . all night! Everyone was happy for the prince, except Gunilla and Lucretia. They were outraged!

Cinderella was having such a good time that she didn't notice when the clock struck six times . . . seven times . . . eight times . . . then suddenly she remembered: At midnight she would be back in her old clothes! The clock struck nine. She pulled herself away from the prince and fled.

"Where are you going?" he called, running after her.

The clock struck ten. Cinderella ran even faster. The clock struck eleven. One of her glass slippers came off but there was no time to stop. The clock struck twelve. She made it to the gate, then disappeared into the shadows. By the time the prince got to the palace gate, she was nowhere in sight.

"Did you see a princess run past here?" he asked one of the guards.

"I've seen no one, sir, except a poor country girl carrying a pumpkin."

The prince looked down and there he saw the glass slipper. He picked it up carefully.

He made a solemn promise. "I will search all of the land to find the owner of this shoe, and when I do, I will make her my bride."

Cinderella returned home in her old clothes, having nothing left of her finery but one of the little slippers, a pumpkin, and a few confused mice scurrying around her feet.

In the morning Cinderella's house was buzzing with activity. Her stepsisters were talking very fast, trying to explain the evening to their mother.

"He says he's going to marry the owner of the shoe," said Gunilla.

"He doesn't even know her name!" said Lucretia.

The wicked stepmother hissed, "Who says she isn't one of you?"

There was a knock on the door. It was the prince and his men. The evil stepmother greeted them with a crooked grin.

"You have come to the right house, my lord, for one of my daughters is your true princess." Gunilla and Lucretia smiled and stepped forward. Each took turns trying to squeeze her feet into the slipper, but it was no use. The slipper was too small for their big feet.

Just as the prince was about to leave, Cinderella shyly asked, "May I try?" The sisters burst into laughter.

"That's our . . . maid," said Lucretia.

"You can ignore her," said Gunilla.

"Yes," the wicked stepmother said, shooting Cinderella a scornful glance, "ignore her!"

But the prince was a man of his word. When he said every girl in the land, he meant it. He knelt to fit the slipper on the girl's foot, and when it slipped on with ease, he knew he had found his bride. To everyone's surprise, Cinderella bashfully produced the other shoe from her pocket!

Everyone was speechless.

In the coming weeks, the entire kingdom prepared for the grandest wedding anyone had ever seen. The poor little cinder maid became a princess and lived happily ever after!

GOLDILOCKS AND THE THREE BEARS

Once upon a time, in a cozy cottage deep in the forest, there lived a family of bears—big, gruff Papa Bear; soft, gentle Mama Bear; and sweet, little Baby Bear.

One morning, Mama Bear made a delicious porridge for breakfast.

"It is too hot," said Papa Bear. "Let's go for a walk in the forest while the porridge cools down."

Soon after they left, a little girl called Goldilocks stumbled upon the Bears' house. She peered in the window and called, "Hello!" When no one answered, she decided to go inside.

Goldilocks spotted the Bears' porridge on the table and took a bite from the biggest bowl. "Ouch!" she cried. "This porridge is much too hot!"

Next, she ate a spoonful from the medium-sized bowl.

"Yuck! This porridge is much too cold."

Goldilocks then tried the porridge in Baby Bear's little bowl.

"Ah," she sighed. "This one is just right!" Goldilocks liked it so much that she ate it all.

With a full tummy, Goldilocks went to the fireplace, where there were three chairs. First she sat in the biggest chair, but it was much too tall. Then she sat in the medium-sized chair, but it was very soft, and she sunk down far too low.

Next she tried the littlest chair of all. "This one is just right!" she said. Just then, Goldilocks heard a creak. Before she could say, "Uh-oh!" the chair snapped in pieces, and Goldilocks tumbled to the floor.

Goldilocks tiptoed upstairs, where she found three tidy beds. She tried the biggest bed, but it was too hard. Next she tried the medium-sized bed, but it was too soft. Finally Goldilocks tried the littlest bed of all. It was just right, and she fell fast asleep.

At that moment, the Bear family returned from their walk.

"What's this?" asked Papa Bear as he looked inside his bowl. "Someone has been eating my porridge!"

"And someone's been eating *my* porridge, too," Mama Bear said in dismay.

"Someone has been eating my porridge, too," cried Baby Bear, "and it's all gone!"

Papa Bear examined his chair by the fireplace. "Someone has been sitting in my chair!" he said.

"And someone has been sitting in *my* chair," Mama Bear exclaimed.

"Someone has been sitting in my chair, too," sobbed Baby Bear, "and now it's broken!"

The three bears went upstairs.

"Someone has been sleeping in my bed!" growled Papa Bear.

"And someone has been sleeping in *my* bed!" added Mama Bear, shaking her head.

"Someone has been sleeping in my bed, too…"
Baby Bear gasped, "and she's still here!"

Goldilocks opened her eyes and was shocked to
find three bears staring back at her.

Terrified, Goldilocks jumped up and ran out of
the cottage.

Baby Bear ran after her, calling, "Don't leave!
Come back! Come and play with me!"

From that day forward, Goldilocks was always
welcome in the Bears' home . . . and they all lived
happily ever after.

Jack and the Beanstalk

Once upon a time, there was a widow who lived in a little cottage with her only son, Jack. Jack was a silly boy but very kindhearted. They were so poor that by the end of a long winter, they were out of food.

"We have no choice," his mother said. "We must sell our cow. Take her to town and make sure to get a fair price."

On his way to town, an old man called out to Jack, "I will trade you that cow for these magic beans."

"I don't know...." said Jack.

"Did you hear me, boy? I said *magic beans*! They are guaranteed to bring you riches beyond your wildest imagination!"

If the beans did what the man said, then Jack's mother would not be so sad. He wanted to make his mother happy and so traded the cow for the beans.

When he returned home and showed his mother the beans, she scolded Jack and shed many tears. "Oh, you foolish boy!" she cried, throwing the beans out the window.

Jack was very sorry but it was too late—there was no food for dinner.

When he woke up, the room looked strange. The sun was shining into it, but the light was green! The beans his mother had thrown into the garden had grown up into a huge beanstalk with leaves so big that they covered the window. The beanstalk grew past the roof of his cottage, past the trees, and disappeared above it!

Climbing it would be easy, thought Jack. And so he did.

At last he reached the top and found himself in front of a gigantic castle.

Jack felt bad about trading the cow for the beans. Perhaps the people of the castle could help him. He crawled beneath the door. Just then a giantess walked into the room carrying a massive loaf of bread. Surely she wouldn't mind sharing it.

"Good morning, ma'am," said Jack. "Would you be so kind as to share your bread?"

The woman tore off a chunk of bread and gave it to Jack. "You'd better leave and forget you ever came to this place," the tall woman said. "If my husband catches you, it is *you* who will be breakfast!"

Just then there was a thumping noise loud as thunder.

"There's my husband now! If he finds you, you are doomed! Quick, you must hide. After breakfast, he always falls asleep. You can sneak out then."

The crashing footsteps were louder and louder until finally, the giant appeared. "Fee-fi-fo-fum, I smell the blood of an Englishman. Let him be alive or let him be dead, I'll grind his bones to make my bread!"

"Don't be silly," said the giantess. "You smell scraps of the boy you ate yesterday. Sit down, have your breakfast, and forget all that Englishman nonsense." The giant's wife set down a platter with enough food to feed one hundred men.

After the giant licked the platter clean, he called to his wife. "Bring me my gold, my hen, and my magic harp!"

His wife brought a big tray into the room. On top sat two tidy stacks of gold coins, a hen in a cage, and a harp.

"Lay!" the giant shouted, and to Jack's amazement, the hen laid a golden egg!

"Play!" the giant shouted and the three women carved in the frame of the harp came to life, singing a sweet and gentle tune. The giant counted his money for a while but the harp's song was so soothing that soon he closed his eyes and nodded off to sleep.

Jack slowly came out of the shadows, afraid to make a sound. He could hear the giant's wife in the pantry while the giant snored at the table. It was then that Jack remembered the words of the old man who gave him the beans: They are guaranteed to bring you riches beyond your wildest imagination. *This must be what the old man meant!* Jack thought.

So he climbed onto the table, filled his pockets with gold, and scooped up the magic hen. He was reaching for the harp when the three women began to shout, "Master! Master!" and the horrible giant awoke.

"Fee-fi-fo-fum!" the giant shouted. "I smell the blood of an Englishman. Let him be alive or let him be dead, I'll grind his bones to make my bread!" The giant looked at the table and saw that the hen and coins were not there. "Who dares to steal from me?" His voice boomed throughout the castle, shook the windows, and rattled the walls.

The ladies of the harp pointed to Jack. The giant lunged, but Jack was quick. He ran as fast as he could toward the beanstalk. The gold coins were so heavy that they tore holes in his pockets and all the coins fell to the floor. He didn't care. As long as Jack had the hen, he and his mother would not starve. He was almost to the beanstalk with the giant fast behind him.

"Fee-fi-fo-fum!" the giant shouted. Jack grabbed hold of the beanstalk with one hand and held the hen in the other. He slid down, down, down to his home.

"I smell the blood of an Englishman!"

Jack reached the bottom of the beanstalk, where his mother was chopping wood. He grabbed the axe and took a swipe at the beanstalk. They could see the giant's shadow coming closer to the ground.

"What is it?" his mother screamed.

"Let him be alive or let him be dead!" The giant continued to climb down the beanstalk, but Jack kept swinging his axe at the stalk. With one last mighty chop of the axe, Jack broke through the vine.

"I'll grind his bones to make my—"

The stalk tipped over and the giant smashed through the soil to the bottom of the earth!

Jack was out of breath. His mother was shocked into silence. There was not a sound at all . . . until the chicken clucked.

"Lay!" Jack ordered. And the chicken laid a golden egg.

"Oh, my dear boy!" the woman cried, giving her son a hug.

CHICKEN LITTLE

Once upon a time, Chicken Little was scratching in her garden when an acorn fell out of a tree and hit her on the head.

"Oh, dear me!" she cried. "The sky is falling. I must go and tell the king!"

So she ran and ran until she met Henny Penny.

"Good morning, Chicken Little," said Henny Penny. "Where are you going?"

"Oh, Henny Penny, the sky is falling, and I am going to tell the king!"

"How do you know the sky is falling?" asked Henny Penny.

"A piece of it fell on my head!" said Chicken Little.

"Then I will go with you," said Henny Penny.

So they ran and ran until they met Turkey Lurkey.

"Good morning, Henny Penny and Chicken Little," said Turkey Lurkey. "Where are the two of you going?"

"Oh, Turkey Lurkey, the sky is falling, and we are going to tell the king!" they said.

"How do you know the sky is falling?" asked Turkey Lurkey.

"Chicken Little told me," said Henny Penny.

"A piece of it fell on my head!" said Chicken Little.

"Then I will go with you," said Turkey Lurkey.

So they ran and ran until they met Ducky Lucky.

"Where are the three of you going?" he asked.

"The sky is falling, and we are going to tell the king," answered Turkey Lurkey.

"How do you know the sky is falling?" asked Ducky Lucky.

"Henny Penny told me," said Turkey Lurkey.

"Chicken Little told me," said Henny Penny.

"A piece of it fell on my head!" said Chicken Little.

"Then I will go with you," said Ducky Lucky.

So they ran and ran until they met Goosey Loosey, on her way to the bakery.

"Where are the four of you going?" she asked.

"The sky is falling, and we are going to tell the king," answered Ducky Lucky.

"How do you know it is falling?" asked Goosey Loosey.

"Turkey Lurkey told me," answered Ducky Lucky.

"Henny Penny told me," said Turkey Lurkey.

"Chicken Little told me," said Henny Penny.

"A piece of it fell on my head!" said Chicken Little.

"Then I will go with you," said Goosey Loosey.

So they ran and ran until they met Foxy Loxy.

"My, my. Look at all these plump birds," he said, licking his lips. "Where is everyone going?"

"The sky is falling, and we are going to tell the king," they all replied together.

"But you are not going the right way," said Foxy Loxy, squinting his wicked eyes. "Shall I show you the way to go?"

"Oh, certainly," they all answered at once and followed Foxy Loxy, until they came to the door of his cave among the rocks.

"This is a short way to the king's palace," said Foxy Loxy.

Just as the little feathered folks were about to follow the fox into his cave, a little gray squirrel jumped out from behind the bushes and whispered to them, "If you go in, that fox will eat all of you!"

The little squirrel threw a big stone and hit the old fox right on the head.

"The sky surely *is* falling," groaned Foxy Loxy, as he fell to the ground. Happy to escape from the wicked fox, the feathered friends thanked the squirrel and continued their journey to see the king.

By and by, they came to the palace where the wise king lived. Upon entering they all shouted at once, "King, we have come to warn you that the sky is falling!"

"How do you know the sky is falling?" asked the king.

"A piece of it fell on my head!" said Chicken Little.

"Come nearer, Chicken Little," said the king and, leaning from his velvet throne, picked the acorn from the feathers of Chicken Little's head. "You see, it was only an acorn and not part of the sky at all," said the king.

Weary but wiser, the little feathered friends left the palace and started on their long journey home.

THE TORTOISE
AND THE HARE

There once was a hare who was always boasting of his speed.

"There is no one in the forest who can run as fast as me," he said, strutting in front of the other animals. "I have never been beaten and I challenge anyone here to race me."

"I accept your challenge," said the tortoise in his slow way.

The hare burst out laughing. "That's a good joke," said the hare. "Why, I can beat you without even trying!"

"Wait until you have won before you start to brag," answered the tortoise.

So the racecourse was laid out, and all the animals gathered to see the start. The hare bounded off in a great burst of speed that left the tortoise far behind in the dust. The hare looked back. He was so far ahead that he could not even see the tortoise anymore.

"I've got plenty of time," the hare said, as he lay down under a big tree beside the road. "I'll let him catch up a little, just to make the finish of the race more exciting."

But as he waited, the hare grew tired. Soon he fell asleep in the shade of the big tree.

Meanwhile, the tortoise was plodding along the hot, dusty road. He came ever so slowly, but he kept right at it. Soon he came upon the hare sleeping by the roadside. The tortoise crawled past the hare without making a sound.

When the hare finally woke up, he could not believe his eyes: The tortoise was just about to reach the finish line! All the animals of the forest cheered wildly. The hare jumped up and ran as fast as he could, but he could not catch up to the slow-moving tortoise.

As the tortoise crossed the finish line, he said, "Slow and steady wins the race." The tortoise was the winner; the hare could never brag again. And all the animals were very glad of that!

The Little Red Hen

Once upon a time, not so very long ago, there was a pig, a duck, a cat, and a little red hen that lived together in a cozy little house.

The pig just wanted to wallow in his juicy mud puddle, the duck just wanted to swim on her little pond, and the cat just wanted to sit in the sun and wash herself with her rough tongue. This left all the work of the house for the busy little red hen.

One day as the little red hen was scratching about in the front yard, she came upon a grain of wheat. That gave her an idea.

"Who will plant this grain of wheat?" she asked.

"Not I," grunted the pig from his puddle.

"Not I," quacked the duck from her pond.

"Not I," purred the cat with a wide yawn.

"Very well, *I* will," said the little red hen. And she did.

The grain of wheat sprouted, and it grew, and it grew until it was tall and golden and ripe.

"Who will cut the wheat?" called the little red hen.

"Not I," grunted the pig from his puddle.

"Not I," quacked the duck from her pond.

"Not I," purred the cat with a flip of her red tongue.

"Very well, *I* will," said the little red hen. And she did.

Soon the grains of wheat were all ready to be ground into flour.

"Who will take the wheat to the mill?" called the little red hen.

"Not I," grunted the pig from his puddle.

"Not I," quacked the duck from her pond.

"Not I," purred the cat with a toss of her head.

"Very well, *I* will," said the little red hen. And she did.

When she returned from the mill with a little sack of wheat flour, she asked, "Who will make the flour into bread?"

"Not I," grunted the pig from his puddle.

"Not I," quacked the duck from her pond.

"Not I," purred the cat, stroking her whiskers.

"Very well, *I* will," said the little red hen. And she did.

Soon the little red hen was taking from the oven the most beautiful loaf of bread.

"Who will eat this bread?"

"I will!" grunted the pig, scrambling up from his puddle.

"I will!" quacked the duck, paddling in from her pond.

"I will!" purred the cat, with one last quick lick at her paws.

"Oh, no, you won't," said the little red hen. "I found the grain of wheat. I planted the seed. I reaped the ripe grains. I took them to the mill. I baked the bread. I shall eat it myself."

And she did.

THE UGLY DUCKLING

One sunny day on a little farm, there was a small pond where a duck was sitting on her nest. Four of the eggs were small, one was much larger than the rest, and all seemed ready to hatch.

The four little eggs cracked open and out popped four little ducklings, yellow as daffodils and pretty as could be. The mother duck was pleased, watching the ducklings peeping about the garden. "Just one more to go," she said, turning her attention to the largest egg of all. But it did not open. So the mama duck waited.

At last the big egg cracked. "Honk, honk!" said the young one. The mother duck gasped, for the largest one was not yellow as a daffodil but an ashy gray. *He must be a turkey*, she thought. *I have an idea. We'll go swimming in the pond. Then I will know for sure.* For every mother duck knows, turkeys cannot swim.

The mother duck went to the water with the five young ones following behind her. She jumped in with a splash. "Quack, quack," she cried. One after another the little ones jumped in. The big one swam the fastest of all.

"Look how well he uses his legs!" said the mother. "That is not a turkey. He is my own child, and he is not so odd after all . . . if you look at him properly."

After their morning swim, the mother duck took her ducklings to the farmyard to introduce them to the other ducks. Everywhere they went, there was whispering.

"Look how ugly that one is!" the other ducks said.

"Leave him alone," the mother duck scolded. "He is a good creature, and he swims more beautifully than the rest."

But the other ducks on the farm continued to tease him, laugh at him, and call him terrible names. One day, the ugly duckling was just too sad to stay on the farm any longer. He squeezed under the gate and, because he hadn't learned to fly yet, he began to walk away.

Toward evening the ugly duckling reached a poor little cottage that seemed ready to collapse, and only remained standing because it could not decide on which side to fall first. The back door was not quite closed, so he slipped inside and went to sleep.

In the morning, the strange visitor was discovered by a tomcat and a hen. The tomcat purred at the duckling and the hen started to cluck.

"Can you lay eggs?" the hen asked.

"No."

"Can you raise your back or purr?" asked the tomcat.

"No."

"Well," the hen said, "what can you do?"

The duckling thought for a while. "I like to swim," he said.

"What an absurd idea," said the hen. "You have nothing else to do, therefore you have foolish fancies. If you could purr or lay eggs, those thoughts would disappear."

"But it is so delightful to swim," said the duckling.

"Delightful, indeed!" said the hen. "Ask the cat— he is the cleverest animal I know—ask him how he would like to swim about on the water! Ask our mistress, the old woman—there is no one in the world more clever than she is. Do you think she would like to swim?"

"You don't understand me," said the duckling.

"Who can understand you, I wonder? Do you consider yourself cleverer than the cat or the old woman? Believe me, I speak only for your own good. I advise you to lay eggs and learn to purr as quickly as possible."

"I think it's time for me to go," said the duckling.

So the duckling left the cottage and soon found a pond where he could swim and dive. But as winter approached, the air grew colder and colder. The duckling had to swim quickly on the water to keep from freezing, but every night the space on which he swam became smaller and smaller.

In the morning, a peasant found the duckling frozen to the ice. He broke the ice and carried the duckling home. The peasant and his wife revived the poor little creature. When the peasant's children wanted to play with him, the duckling was frightened. He started up in terror and flew all around the kitchen, knocking over jars of food. The woman shooed the duckling through the open door, and he endured a hard winter all alone.

When spring came, the ugly duckling saw that everything around him had become beautiful. He raised his wings, and, to his delight, he was flying! He rose high into the air and flew until he reached a large garden with a lovely lake. Just in front of him he saw three beautiful swans swimming lightly over the smooth water. The duckling felt more unhappy than ever.

"I want to make friends with them, but I know they will not have me because I am too ugly." Though he was afraid they would reject him, the duckling could not help but swim toward the beautiful strangers. He tried to hide his face by keeping his head bowed, but there, in the reflection of the water, he saw the most curious thing: Another swan was staring back at him. Why, it was him! He was a swan, too. The other swans rushed to meet him with outstretched wings. They stroked his neck with their bills, for this is the way swans say, "Hello."

Soon a boy and a girl came into the garden with corn and pieces of bread, which they threw into the water.

"Look!" shouted the boy. "There is a new one!"

The girl said, "And he is the most beautiful of all!"

The newest swan rustled his feathers and cried out to the boy and girl with joy. And that is the story of the ugly duckling who became a swan.

THE THREE LITTLE PIGS

Once upon a time, there were three little pigs who lived in a cozy house with their mother.

One day the mother pig said, "You are all grown up now. It is time to go out into the world and build your own houses. Build them strong so you will be safe from the big, bad wolf."

The first little pig was a lazy little pig. He built the simplest kind of house so he could have time to rest. He made a house of straw. It was not very strong.

The second little pig was a playful little pig. He built his house quickly so he could go out and play. His house was made of sticks. It was not very strong.

The third little pig was a smart little pig. He listened carefully to his mother's advice and built a very strong house of bricks.

The three little pigs didn't know that lurking in the nearby forest was the big, bad wolf. The wolf was hungry, and for his supper he wanted a pig!

The big, bad wolf came and knocked on the first little pig's door.

"Little pig, little pig, let me come in!" he roared.

"Not by the hair on my chinny-chin-chin," replied the first pig.

"Then I'll huff and I'll puff and I'll blow your house in!" So the wolf huffed and he puffed—and he blew the straw house down. The first little pig ran away as fast as his legs could take him.

Next, the wolf knocked on the second little pig's door. "Little pig, little pig, let me come in!" he roared.

"Not by the hair on my chinny-chin-chin!" said the second little pig.

"Then I'll huff and I'll puff and I'll blow your house in!"

So the wolf huffed and he puffed—and he blew the stick house down. The second little pig ran away as fast as his legs could take him.

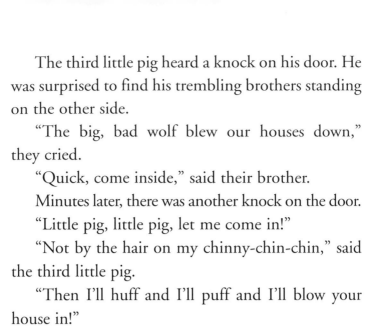

The third little pig heard a knock on his door. He was surprised to find his trembling brothers standing on the other side.

"The big, bad wolf blew our houses down," they cried.

"Quick, come inside," said their brother.

Minutes later, there was another knock on the door.

"Little pig, little pig, let me come in!"

"Not by the hair on my chinny-chin-chin," said the third little pig.

"Then I'll huff and I'll puff and I'll blow your house in!"

So he huffed and he puffed, then he puffed and he huffed, but no matter how hard he tried, he could not blow the brick house down.

The big, bad wolf was very angry. "I'll get you, little piggies!" he snarled. He climbed up on the roof and crept toward the chimney.

Hearing the wolf on the roof, the third little pig was quick to light a fire. When the wolf slid down the chimney, he was met with hot, crackling flames.

The wolf's tail was badly scorched. He ran out of the house into the woods, howling. The big, bad wolf never bothered the three little pigs again . . . and they lived happily ever after!

The Princess and the Pea

Once upon a time, there was a prince who was looking for a wife. Since he was a prince, his wife would have to be a princess. He traveled all over the land to find one, but each time he met a princess there was something disagreeable about her. Princess Beatrix was very picky, and Princess Flora was always sad. Princess Francesca was very messy, and Princess Delia had too many cats. So the prince returned from his travels without a princess of his own.

One evening there was a terrible storm. Thunder shook the castle and lightning lit up the sky. Suddenly, there was a knock on the gate. The guard opened the door, and outside stood a soaking wet girl.

"Please let me in," she said. "I am Princess Amelia, and I've lost my way."

The guard fetched the royal family to meet this bedraggled stranger. Was she really a princess? At that moment the prince did not care, for he thought this strange girl was lovely. The queen did not feel the same way.

I bet she is an ordinary girl looking to marry my son, thought the queen. This gave her an idea. "Why don't you stay here for the night, my dear," she said to Amelia.

As Amelia took a hot bath and changed into a warm nightgown, the queen searched the pantry for a hard, dried pea. With the help of her servants, the queen took the mattress off the bed and laid a pea on the bottom. Twenty soft mattresses were then laid upon the pea.

The queen explained her plan to the king. "Only a real princess will be able to feel a pea through twenty mattresses," she said.

At breakfast time the queen asked Amelia how she had slept. At first Amelia did not say anything for she didn't want to be impolite. But when the queen asked her a second and then a third time, the young girl finally told the truth.

"Heaven only knows what was in the bed," she said. "It was so uncomfortable. I tossed and turned all night!"

The royal family was overjoyed: Amelia was a real princess, indeed! The prince and princess were married soon after. As for the pea, it was put in a glass case in the palace museum, and you can see it there to this day!